T A

O. HENRY

RETOLD TIMELESS CLASSICS

Perfection Learning®

Retold by Peg Hall

Editor: Susan C. Thies
Illustrator: Greg Hargreaves
Designer: Tobi Cunningham

For information, contact
Perfection Learning® Corporation
1000 North Second Avenue, P.O. Box 500
Logan, Iowa 51546-0500
perfectionlearning.com
Phone: 800-831-4190 • Fax: 712-644-2392
Reinforced Library Binding ISBN-13: 978-0-7569-0314-5
Reinforced Library Binding ISBN-10: 0-7569-0314-9
Paperback ISBN-13: 978-0-7891-5529-0
Paperback ISBN-10: 0-7891-5529-X
7 8 9 10 11 PP 12 11 10 09 08
perfectionlearning.com
Printed in the U.S.A.

Table of Contents

The Cop and the Anthem

A dead leaf fell in Soapy's lap. He moved uneasily on the bench. The leaf was Jack Frost's calling card. It was a warning that winter was coming to New York City. Soapy knew he had to think about the coming cold weather. And that was why he moved uneasily.

Soapy's thoughts were not of warm Southern skies. No, he was thinking of jail. Three months in a cell were what he wanted. Three months of being fed and having a warm place to sleep. To Soapy, that seemed like heaven.

He knew the time had come. Three newspapers had not been enough to keep him warm the night before. He had shivered as he slept on his bench in the square. So thoughts of jail filled Soapy's mind. He had no interest in a shelter or any other form of charity. There were all kinds of places that people like Soapy could go. But he had found that charity had its cost. The price might be a bath or an endless round of questions. So Soapy had long ago decided that jail was a better choice. When he was a guest of the law, his private affairs could stay private.

Now Soapy had to find a way to get thrown into jail. There were many possibilities. The most pleasant was to go to a fine restaurant and eat an expensive meal. And then to say that he had no money. He would be handed over to a policeman, and a judge would do the rest.

Soapy left his bench and strolled out onto the street. He turned up Broadway and stopped at a glittering restaurant. It was the kind of place where only the best people ate.

Soapy figured he looked fine from the vest upward. He had shaved. His coat was neat and clean. And he was wearing a black tie that had been given to him by a kind lady. He just had to get to a table and sit down. The part of him that would show would raise no doubt in a waiter's mind.

Roast duck, thought Soapy. That was what he would order. And then some cheese and coffee to finish the meal. That way he would be full and happy for the trip to jail.

Soapy walked into the restaurant. At once, the waiter's eye went to Soapy's torn pants and dirty shoes. Strong hands turned him around and showed him to the sidewalk. It seemed that a good meal was not going to be Soapy's way to jail. He had to come up with another plan.

At the corner of Sixth Avenue, Soapy spotted a well-lit store. He picked up a stone and threw it through the window. People came running around the corner, a policeman in the lead. Soapy stood still, his hands in his pockets. He smiled at the sight of the policeman.

"Where's the man who did it?" asked the officer.

"Don't you think I might have something to do with it?" asked Soapy.

The policeman couldn't believe that. Men who smash windows don't wait around to talk to the police. They take to their heels.

The policeman saw a man halfway down the block. The gentleman was running after a cat. The policeman started after him. Soapy sighed and started to walk again.

On the other side of the street was a restaurant. This was no fancy place. It served large amounts of food at cheap prices. Its dishes were thick and its soup and napkins thin.

Soapy walked inside and sat down. He ordered steak, flapjacks, doughnuts, and pie. Then he told the waiter that he had no money.

"Now, get busy and call a cop," said Soapy. "And don't keep a gentleman waiting."

"No cop for you," said the waiter. "Hey, Con!" he called to another waiter.

The two fellows tossed Soapy on the sidewalk outside. Slowly he unfolded himself and got to his feet. He beat the dust from his clothes. Arrest seemed only a dream. Jail seemed very far away.

Soapy traveled five more blocks before he had the nerve to try again. This time he was sure he would succeed. A young woman was standing in front of a shop window. Two yards away, a policeman leaned against a wall.

Soapy's plan was to bother the woman. He was sure the policeman would come and haul him off to jail.

So he straightened his tie and tipped his hat at an angle. Then he walked close to the young woman. He smiled, then started to talk to her in an unpleasant way. With half an eye, Soapy watched the policeman. The young woman only had to call out, "This man is bothering me!" The policeman would come at once.

Instead, the young woman smiled back at Soapy. She reached out and grabbed his coat sleeve. "Why, Mike," she said. "It's good to see you. Are you going to buy me dinner?" She held tightly to his arm as they walked past the policeman.

As soon as they turned the corner, Soapy shook off her arm and started to run. He didn't stop until he had reached a lighted section of town. Women in fur coats and men in top hats were everywhere. And a policeman stood in front of a theater.

Soapy had an idea. He would get arrested for "disturbing the peace." He started to yell. He danced, howled, raved, and otherwise made noise.

The policeman turned to a gentleman and said, "He's a college lad. Celebrating a winning game. We've been told to let them be."

Poor Soapy! At once he gave up making noise. Would no policeman arrest him? Jail was beginning to seem like an impossible goal. He buttoned his thin coat against the cold wind.

Then Soapy saw a well-dressed man nearby. His silk umbrella was leaning by a shop door. Soapy stepped up, took the umbrella, and walked off with it. The man followed him.

"My umbrella," he said.

"Oh, is it?" asked Soapy. "Well, why don't you call a policeman? There's one right over there."

The umbrella owner slowed his steps. Soapy did the same, suddenly thinking that this plan, too, was going to fail.

"Of course," said the umbrella man. "That is—well, mistakes happen. If it's your umbrella, please forgive me. I found it in a restaurant this morning. If you're sure it's yours—"

The ex-umbrella man walked off. Soapy was upset. He walked eastward, toward a section where the roads were torn up. He tossed the umbrella away. He muttered about policemen who didn't do their jobs. He wanted to be arrested, and they thought he could do no wrong.

At last Soapy reached a quiet street. He turned and started to walk back toward the square. Back to his home on the park bench.

On a quiet street, Soapy came to a standstill. An old church stood before him. A soft light glowed though one purple-stained window. And sweet music drifted outside. It kept Soapy there. He leaned against the iron fence to listen.

The moon was shining above. There were few cars or people. Sparrows sang softly in the branches. Soapy felt as if he were in a country churchyard rather than the city. And the music! It was a song he had known long ago. Back when his life included things like mothers and roses and friends and clean thoughts and clothing.

A wonderful change came over Soapy. All at once he saw how far he had fallen. How bad his life had become. He was overcome with a new thought. He would pull himself out of the mud. He would make a man of himself again. He would do battle with the evil that had taken hold of him. There was time. He was still young. Tomorrow he would find a job. He would be somebody in the world. He would—

Soapy felt a rough hand on his arm. He turned and looked into the face of a policeman.

"What are you doing hanging around here?" asked the officer.

"Nothing," said Soapy.

"Then come along," said the policeman.

"Three months in jail," said the judge the next morning.

The Gift of the Magi

Only $1.87. That was all. And 60 cents of it was in pennies. Pennies saved one and two at a time. Saved by buying old vegetables and stale bread.

Three times Della counted the money. Still $1.87. And tomorrow would be Christmas. There was nothing to do but flop down on the shabby couch and weep. So Della did it. Which makes you think that life is made up of tears and smiles. But mostly tears.

While the lady of the house is getting over her sadness, let's take a look at her home. She lived in a rented flat for $8 a week. It wasn't unbearable, but it wasn't very good either.

In the entryway below, there was a letter box. It was too small to hold a letter. There was also a doorbell. But it didn't work. Above the doorbell was a card that read "Mr. James Dillingham Young."

The "Dillingham" part had seemed fine when its owner was making $30 a week. Now that he wasn't, the letters looked blurred. It was as if they were thinking of shrinking and becoming just a "D." But every time Mr. James Dillingham Young came home, he was called "Jim." And he was hugged by Mrs. James Dillingham Young. You have already met her as Della.

Now Della finished her cry. She looked out the window. A gray cat was walking on a gray fence in a gray backyard. Tomorrow was Christmas Day. And she only had $1.87 for Jim's gift. She had been saving for months, but $20 a week doesn't go far. Things like food and rent cost a lot. So she only had $1.87 to buy a present for Jim. Her Jim.

She had spent many happy hours planning what to get him. Something fine and rare and silver. Something good enough to belong to Jim. Suddenly Della turned and looked into a mirror that hung on the wall. Her eyes were shining, but her face was white. She pulled the pins out of her hair and let it hang down.

There were two things that James Dillingham Young looked upon with pride. One was his gold watch. It had belonged to his father and grandfather. The other was Della's hair. To Jim, both were treasures. The gold watch was fine enough for a king. And Della's hair was more beautiful than any queen's could be.

Now Della's hair fell about her like a shiny brown waterfall. It reached below her knees and covered her like a cloak.

Then Della quickly pinned her hair back on top of her head. When she was done, she stood in the middle of the room for a moment. A tear or two splashed on the worn old rug.

On went her old brown jacket. On went her old brown hat. With a whirl of skirts, she went out the door. She hurried down the stairs to the street.

Della didn't stop until she reached a small shop. A sign outside said "Madam Sophia. Hair Goods of All Kinds." Della almost ran into the shop, where a tall, white-faced woman waited. She hardly looked like a "Sophia."

"Will you buy my hair?" asked Della.

"I do buy hair," said Madam. "Take off your hat, and let's have a look at it."

Off went the hat. Down went the shiny waterfall of hair.

"Twenty dollars," said Madam.

"Give it to me quick," said Della.

Oh, the next two hours flew by on rosy wings. Della went from shop to shop, looking for the perfect gift.

She found it at last. She was sure that it had been made for Jim and no one else. It was a watch chain. It had a simple, elegant design that spoke of value—as is true of all good things. It was worthy of Jim's watch. As soon as she saw it, Della knew it had to be Jim's.

Twenty-one dollars was what it cost. Della paid for it and hurried home with the 87 cents. With that chain on his watch, Jim would be proud to check the time anywhere. Grand as the watch was, he sometimes kept it out of sight. The old leather strap he used in place of a chain was worn and ugly.

When Della got home, her excitement gave way to reason. She had to do something about her hacked-off hair. She heated her curling irons and went to work. She had to repair the damages done in the name of love. Which is always a big task, my friends. A huge task.

Within 40 minutes her head was covered with tiny curls. They made her look something like a schoolboy. She checked herself in the mirror.

"I hope Jim doesn't get mad when he first sees me," she said. "I think I look rather like a chorus girl. But what else could I do? I couldn't buy him a thing with $1.87!"

At 7:00 the coffee was made. The frying pan was at the back of the stove. It was hot and ready to cook the pork chops.

Jim was never late. Della hid the watch chain in her hand. She sat on the corner of the table near the door. Then she heard his footsteps down below. She turned white for just a moment. "Please let him think I am still pretty," she said to herself.

The door opened and Jim stepped in. He looked thin and very serious. Poor fellow—he was only 22. So young to have a family! He had no overcoat and no gloves.

Jim stopped at the door like a dog that had scented a game bird. His eyes were on Della. There was a look in them that she couldn't read. A look that frightened her. It wasn't anger, or surprise, or horror, or anything she had thought it might be. He simply stared at her with a strange expression on his face.

Della slid off the table and went to him. "Jim, darling," she cried, "don't look at me that way. I had my hair cut off because I wanted to buy you a gift. You don't mind, do you? I just had to do it. My hair grows fast, you know. So say 'Merry Christmas,' and let's be happy. You have no idea what a wonderful gift I have for you."

"You cut off your hair?" asked Jim. He asked the question as if he didn't already know the answer.

"Cut it off and sold it," said Della. "Don't you like me just as well, anyhow? It's still me, after all."

Jim looked around the room. "You say your hair is gone?"

"There's no reason to look for it here," said Della. "It's gone, I tell you. I sold it. Now, it's Christmas Eve. Be nice to me. I sold it for you."

Then a sweet look came over her face. "My hair may be gone, Jim, but nobody could take my love for you."

Jim seemed to wake up. He put his arms around Della. For ten seconds, let us leave them alone and look in the other direction. Eight dollars a week or a million a year. What's the difference?

Now Jim pulled a package from his pocket and put it on the table. "Don't get me wrong, Della," he said. "Nothing you did to your hair could make me love you less. But if you unwrap that package, you'll see why you had me going."

Della tore at the paper and string with white fingers. When she saw what was inside, she gave a cry of joy. And then, alas! A quick change to weeping and wailing. Jim had to use all his powers to comfort her.

For there lay a set of hair combs. Combs that Della had often looked at in a shop window. Beautiful combs with jeweled rims. Just the thing to wear in her long, lovely hair. They cost a lot, she knew. She had looked at them without ever thinking she could own them. And now, they were hers. But she had no long hair to put them in.

Still, she hugged the combs to her. At last she looked up at Jim and smiled. "My hair grows so fast, Jim," she said.

Then Della jumped up, saying, "Oh, oh!" Jim hadn't seen his beautiful present. She held it out to him on her hand. The dull metal seemed to reflect her smile.

"Isn't it wonderful, Jim? I hunted all over town to find it. You'll have to check the time a hundred times a day now. Give me your watch. I want to see how it looks with the chain."

Instead of giving her the watch, Jim sank down on the couch. "Della, let's put our gifts away for a while. They're too nice to use right now. I sold the watch to get the money to buy the combs. And now, let's eat dinner."

The magi, as you know, were wise men. They brought gifts to the baby in the manger. They invented the art of giving Christmas gifts. Being wise, they probably gave wise gifts. And here I have told you a tale of two foolish young people. They both unwisely gave up their greatest treasures. But here is a last word to the wise. Let it be said that of all who give and receive gifts, Della and Jim were the wisest. They are the magi.

The Princess and the PUMA

There had to be a king and queen, of course. The king was an awful old man. He wore six-shooters and spurs. He shouted in such a loud voice that the rattlesnakes would run into their holes. Before he was a king, they called him "Whispering Ben." Then he came to own 50,000 acres of land and more cattle than he could count. So they called him "Ben O'Donnell, the Cattle King."

The queen had been a Mexican girl. She made a good wife for Ben. She even got him to lower his voice in the house. At least enough to keep the dishes from getting broken. When Ben first got to be king, she would sit on the porch of Espinosa Ranch. She would weave simple rugs. But then the money got hard to ignore. Comfortable chairs and a big table were brought to the ranch. She bowed her smooth, dark head and put up with it all.

You have met the king and queen first. However, they do not really matter to this story. It could be called "The Story of the Princess, the Happy Thought, and the Mexican Lion."

Josefa O'Donnell was the princess. From her mother, she got her warm nature and her dark beauty. From her father, she got bravery, common sense, and the ability to rule. The combination was worth going miles to see. Josefa could shoot five out of six bullets through a can swinging on a string. And she could do it while riding her pony at a gallop. She would play for hours with her white kitten. She could do numbers in her head. Things like what 1,545 colts would cost at $8.50 a head.

Espinosa Ranch was huge. But Josefa had ridden over every mile of it. Every cowboy on

the range knew her by sight. Ripley Givens, a
foreman on the ranch, had seen her one day. At
once he made up his mind to marry her.
Impossible? No. In those days, a man was a man.
After all, being called "Cattle King" does not
mean you have royal blood. Often it just means
that you are skilled in the art of cattle stealing.

One day Ripley Givens rode over to another
ranch on some business. He was late setting out on
his return trip. It was sundown when he reached
White Horse Crossing. He still had 16 miles to go
and he was tired. So he decided to spend the night
at the crossing.

It was a fine enough spot. The riverbank was
covered with trees and bushes. Not far away was a
stretch of grass. It would be supper for his horse
and a bed for Givens.

He tied his horse to a branch. Then he spread
out his saddle blankets to dry. He sat down with
his back against a tree.

Then there was a sudden, shivering wail from
somewhere in the trees. The horse danced at the
end of his rope and snorted with fear. Givens
reached for his gunbelt, which lay on the grass. A
great fish jumped in the water. A little brown
rabbit twitched his whiskers. The horse went on
eating grass.

It's a good idea to be careful when a Mexican lion sings at sundown. His song may mean that he can't find any young calves or fat lambs. And that he wants to meet *you.*

In the grass, there was an empty fruit can. Givens caught sight of it and grunted happily. He had a handful or two of ground coffee in his coat pocket. Hot coffee! What cowboy could want more?

In two minutes, he had a fire going. He picked up the can and started for the water. He was almost there when he saw something. A pony was eating grass a little bit to his left. And Josefa O'Donnell was just getting to her feet at the edge of the river. She had been drinking. Now she brushed sand from her hands.

Ten yards away, to her right, Givens saw the Mexican lion. It was crouching, half hidden by the bushes. Its yellow eyes glared hungrily. Six feet behind those eyes, the tip of the lion's tail stretched out straight. The beast was ready to leap!

Givens did what he could. His six-shooter was 35 yards away. He yelled and ran between the lion and the princess.

What happened next was fast and somewhat confused. As Givens tackled the lion, he saw a streak in the air. He heard a few faint cracks. Then

100 pounds of Mexican lion landed on his head and flattened him. He remembered calling out, "Let up, now! No fair!" Then he crawled out from under the lion. His mouth was full of dirt. He had a big lump on the back of his head where it had hit a tree root.

The lion lay on the grass without moving. Givens was angry. He shook his fist and yelled at the lion. "I'll fight you again!" Then he got hold of himself.

Josefa was standing nearby, quietly reloading her pistol. It hadn't been a difficult shot. A lion makes an easier target than a can swinging on a string. There was a teasing smile on her mouth and in her dark eyes.

The would-be knight felt like a fool. Here had been his chance—the chance he had dreamed of. But instead of looking like a hero, he looked like a clown.

"Is that you, Mr. Givens?" asked Josefa sweetly. "You nearly spoiled my shot when you yelled. Did you hurt your head?"

"Oh, no, that didn't hurt," said Givens quietly. He bent down and dragged his best hat out from under the lion. It was crushed and wrinkled. Then he knelt down. He softly stroked the head of the dead lion.

"Poor old Bill!" he said sadly.

"What?" asked Josefa.

"Of course, you didn't know, Miss Josefa," said Givens. He gave her a look that was half sadness and half forgiveness. "Nobody can blame you. I tried to save him. But I couldn't let you know in time."

"Save who?"

"Why, Bill. I've been looking for him all day. He's been our camp pet for two years. Poor old fellow, he wouldn't have hurt a rabbit. The boys will be upset when they hear about this. But you didn't know that Bill just wanted to play with you."

Josefa's black eyes burned into him. However, Ripley Givens met the test. He stood there, running his fingers through his yellow-brown curls. In his eyes and on his face was a look of sorrow.

"What was your pet doing here?" asked Josefa.

"He ran away yesterday," answered Givens. "It's a wonder the coyotes didn't scare him to death. You see, someone brought a puppy into our camp last week. The pup made things hard for Bill. He'd chase him around and chew on his hind legs. Every night at bedtime, Bill would sneak under one of the boys' blankets. He wanted to get away from the pup. And then he ran away. It's hard to believe. Old Bill was always afraid to get out of sight of the camp."

Josefa looked at the body of the fierce animal. Slowly a red flush came over her cheeks. She lowered her eyes and said, "I'm very sorry. But he looked so big. And he jumped so high that—"

"Poor old Bill was hungry," said Givens. "We always made him jump for his supper in camp. He would lie down and roll over for a piece of meat. He just thought you were going to feed him."

Suddenly Josefa's eyes opened wide. "I might have shot you!" she cried. "You came right between us. You risked your life to save your pet! That was fine, Mr. Givens. I like a man who is kind to animals."

"I've always loved them," said he. "Horses, dogs, Mexican lions, cows, alligators—"

"I hate alligators!" said Josefa. "They're crawly, muddy things!"

"Did I say alligators? I meant antelopes, of course."

Josefa put out her hand. There was a bright, unshed tear in each of her eyes. "Please forgive me, Mr. Givens. I'm only a girl. I was frightened at first. I'm very, very sorry I shot Bill."

Givens took her hand. He held on to it until it was clear that he had forgiven her. "Don't speak of it again, Miss Josefa. It was enough to frighten any young lady. The way Bill looked! I'll explain it to the boys."

"Are you sure you don't hate me?" Josefa moved closer. Her eyes were sweet—begging for forgiveness. "I would hate it if someone killed my kitten. How brave and kind of you to risk being shot to save your pet! How very few men would have done that!"

Foolishness turned to bravery! A clown into a hero! Good for you, Ripley Givens!

It was almost dark now. Of course Miss Josefa couldn't ride on to the ranch alone. Givens put the saddle back on his horse. Then Givens and Josefa rode off together. Side by side they galloped across the grass. The princess and the man who was kind to animals. Flowers bloomed thick around them. Coyotes yelped. Nothing to fear. And yet—

Josefa rode closer. Her little hand reached out. Givens found it with his own.

"I never was frightened before," she said. "But just think! How awful it would be to meet a really wild lion! I'm so glad you came with me."

Ben O'Donnell was sitting on the porch when they got to the ranch. "Is that you, Rip?" he shouted.

"He rode with me, Dad," said Josefa. "I lost my way and it was late."

"Thanks, Rip," said the cattle king. "Stay here tonight and go back to camp in the morning."

But Givens wouldn't do that. He said good night and rode away.

An hour later, Josefa called out to her father. "Say, Pop, you know that old lion they call the Notch-Eared Devil? The one that killed about 50 calves? Well, I took care of him over at White Horse Crossing. Shot him while he was jumping. I knew him by the slice in his left ear. You couldn't have made a better shot yourself, Daddy."

"Good for you!" thundered Whispering Ben.

Bulger's Friend

Many folks thought it was funny when Bulger joined the Salvation Army. The strange old man was the town's odd "character." He lived in a hut he had made himself of scrap wood, tin, canvas, and iron.

Bulger didn't like visitors. So even the bravest boys in town stayed away from his hut. Everyone said the old man was crazy. That he was some kind of wizard. That he was a miser with lots of gold buried in or near his hut. Bulger worked at odd jobs. He weeded gardens and painted fences. He collected scrap metal and old bottles.

One rainy night, the Salvation Army was holding one of its regular meetings. Bulger appeared and asked if he could join. Now, the Salvation Army is known for accepting just about anyone. So the sergeant in charge welcomed the old man.

At once Bulger was given a job as a drummer. It may be that the sergeant thought Bulger would be a sign of the Salvation Army's good works.

So every night, Bulger joined the march from Salvation Army Hall to the street corner. He would stumble along with his drum. As the others played, he would whack the drum soundly. He managed to keep time with the drum, but not with his feet. He would shuffle and stagger and rock from side to side.

Truly, Bulger was not pleasant to watch. He was a bent, clumsy old man. His face was twisted to one side and wrinkled like a prune. He wore a red shirt, the uniform of all members of the Salvation Army. But his fit poorly. It had once belonged to a huge man who had died some time before. So it hung on Bulger's thin body in folds. His old brown cap was always pulled down over one eye. His clothing and his strange walk made him seem like some sort of ape. An ape captured and forced to perform to music.

At the army's street-corner services, folks often bothered Bulger. They called upon him to talk about how he had been saved. They made fun of the way he played the drum. But the old man paid no attention to them. He almost never spoke except to say hello and good-bye to other members of the army.

The sergeant had met many odd characters in his life. So he knew how to handle them. He left Bulger alone for a time. Every evening, the old man would appear at the hall. He'd march up the street and back again. Then he'd put his drum in the corner where it belonged. He'd sit on the last bench at the back of the hall until the meeting was over.

One night the sergeant followed Bulger outside. He put his hand on the old man's shoulder. "Is it well with you?" he asked.

"Not yet, Sergeant," said Bulger. "But I'm trying. I'm glad you came outside. I've been wanting to ask you something. Do you think the Lord would take in a man who comes to him late? A man who's lost everything? Home and friends and money. Wouldn't it look bad to wait till then to come to the Lord?"

"Not at all," said the sergeant. "It doesn't matter to the Lord. The poorer, the more miserable—the greater his love."

"Well, I'm awful poor and miserable," said Bulger. "You know when I can think best, Sergeant? It's when I'm beating the drum. Other times there's a kind of roaring in my head. The drum seems to calm it. That's a thing I'm trying to figure out."

"Do you pray, my friend?" asked the sergeant.

"No, I don't," answered Bulger. "What's the use? Doesn't it say somewhere that a man has to give up his family and friends? That is, if he wants to serve the Lord."

"Only if they stand in his way."

"Well, I've got no family," said the old man. "And only one friend. But it's that friend that has driven me to ruin."

"Free yourself!" cried the sergeant. "He is no friend. He is an enemy that stands between you and the Lord."

"No, he's not an enemy," said Bulger. "He's the best friend I ever had. He keeps me in rags and living on scraps. And yet I never had a better friend. You don't understand, Sergeant. See if you lose all your friends but one, then you'll know you have to hold on to the last one."

"If this friend stands between you and peace, give him up."

"I can't," said the old man. "But you just let me keep on beating the drum. And maybe I will give him up some time. I come so near to thinking it out when I'm hitting that drum. You'll give me more time, won't you?"

"All the time you want," said the sergeant. "Pound away until you hit the right note."

After that, the sergeant would often stop to talk to Bulger. "Knocked that friend of yours out yet?" he'd ask. The answer was always no.

In the South, the winter of 1892 was one to remember. It was far colder than normal. Snow fell many inches deep where it had hardly ever fallen before. There was much suffering among the poor.

The Salvation Army had always been a place to go when there was trouble. Storm, fire, or flood—the members of this small band would help. They would go out and help people who had never learned to beg. But this winter there was more trouble than the army could handle.

At the end of three weeks of cold, a foot of snow fell. Hunger and cold were everywhere. More than 100 women, children, and old men were brought into the hall. There they were warmed and fed. Each day, the soldiers of the Salvation Army went out. They gathered pennies and dimes and quarters to buy food for the needy. They went to the homes of the rich to ask for food and clothing.

The cold stretched on for days. Business was bad in town. The pennies and dimes and quarters stopped coming. Still, the stove in the big hall was kept burning. The long table always held coffee and bread and cheese. But then the money was all gone.

It was almost Christmas. There were 50 children staying in the hall. And there were many other needy children outside in the town. To them, the only joy Christmas had ever brought had come from the Salvation Army. So now the children began to talk about the Christmas tree. Every year, the army had a tree and gifts for the children of the poor.

The sergeant was upset. He knew that not having a tree would break the children's hearts. It would be worse than being cold or hungry. But there was nothing he could do. There was no money for a tree or gifts.

On the night of December 20, the sergeant decided to tell the children there would be no tree. It seemed unfair to let them get their hopes up.

The evening was cold. More snow fell on top of what already lay on the ground. A fierce wind blew from the north. The sergeant entered the hall and took off his thin coat. Soon after that, everyone else drifted in. The women took off their heavy shawls. The men stamped the snow off their feet.

They all sat down to a poor supper of cold meat, beans, and bread. Then they had a short service with song and prayer.

Bulger sat in the shadows at the back. For weeks he hadn't been able to play the drum. The army had been too busy for marching. Still he came to the hall every night and ate with the others. He always left early, going to spend the night in his hut.

The sergeant stood up and rapped on the table. When the room became quiet, he began his talk. He rambled a bit, unlike his usual direct speech. The children had gathered around him in a wiggling and wide-awake circle. They knew he was going to talk about the Christmas tree.

They listened hopefully. The sergeant saw this and swallowed hard. Then he went on talking. He dashed the hope from each little heart. He watched the light fade from their eyes.

There would be no tree. Doing without was nothing new to these children. Still, a few of them sobbed aloud. Their mothers tried to comfort them. A kind of voiceless wail went around the room. It was the ghost of a cry for childish fun they had never known.

Bulger rose and left the room. He was heard fumbling in the little room near the door. Suddenly a thundering roar filled the building.

The sergeant laughed. "It's only Bulger," he said. "Doing a little thinking in his quiet way."

The wind rattled the windows and threw itself around the corners. The sergeant put more coal into the stove. The children were slowly getting over their broken hopes. The women were getting things set up for the night.

Soon it was eight o'clock. The sergeant got ready for his long, cold trip home. Suddenly the door opened and Bulger came in covered with snow. The old man shuffled down the hall to the sergeant. He pulled a wet, dirty bag from under his coat and put it on the table. "Open it," he said.

The sergeant smiled, then picked up the bag and turned it over. His smile turned to a look of amazement. A pile of gold and silver coins had fallen out.

"Count it," said Bulger.

The clink of money was the only sound in the room. That and the howl of the wind outside. The sergeant slowly put the coins into piles.

"Six hundred," he said at last. "Six hundred and twenty-three dollars and eighty-five cents."

"Eighty," said Bulger. "You made a mistake. You're off by five cents. I've thought it out at last, Sergeant. And I've decided to give up that friend I told you about. That's him there. Dollars and cents. Folks were right when they said I was a miser. Take it, Sergeant. Spend it the best way for those that need it. But don't forget a Christmas tree for the young ones. And—"

"Hooray!" cried the sergeant.

"And a new drum," added Bulger.

Then the sergeant made another speech.

Round the Circle

"Did you find what you needed, Sam?" asked Mrs. Webber. She sat in a chair under the oak tree. A paperback book kept her company.

"Yep," answered Sam. "It's perfect, Marthy. At first I was goin' to kick up a fuss because the buttons was all off. But the buttonholes is all busted out too. So I reckon I can't say the buttons is any great loss."

41

"Oh, just put on your necktie," said his wife. "That'll keep the shirt together."

Sam Webber's sheep ranch was in the loneliest part of the country. It was a two-room building that looked like a box. It stood on a gentle hill in the middle of a wilderness of bushes. In front of the house was a small clearing. The sheep sheds stood there, only a few feet from the thorny jungle.

Sam was going to ride over to the Chapman ranch to see about buying some sheep. This was an important business trip. That's why Sam wanted to dress up some. The result wasn't so wonderful. He had managed to change himself from a graceful sheepherder into something much less pleasing. The tight, white collar of his shirt cut into Sam's neck. Without buttons, the shirt looked odd under his vest. His suit fit poorly. And his face wore an expression you'd expect to see on a jailed prisoner.

Sam gave Randy, his three-year-old son, a pat on the head. Then he hurried out to Mexico, his favorite horse.

Marthy rocked in her chair. She put her finger in the book to keep her place. Then she smiled at the picture Sam made in his fancy clothes. "Well, I must say it, Sam," she said. "You look like one of them hayseeds in the picture papers. Not like a Texas sheepman."

"You're the one that ought to blush to say so," said Sam. "You should be tending to your man's clothes. Instead, you're always settin' around readin' them stupid novels."

"Oh, quiet down and ride along," said Mrs. Webber. "You're always fussin' about my reading. I do plenty of work around here. So I'll read when I want to. I live in the wilds here like a varmint. I never see or hear nothin'. So what kind of fun can I have? Not listenin' to you talk, for sure. All you do is complain, complain. One day after another. Go on, Sam, and leave me in peace."

Sam gave his pony a squeeze with his knees. They headed down the trail that ran between the ranch and the road. It was eight o'clock and already very warm. He should have started three hours earlier. The Chapman ranch was only 18 miles away. But there was no road that went right there. He would have to ride through some wild country. Sam had gone there once before. However, that was with a cowhand from the ranch to show him the way. Still, he was sure he knew how to get there.

Some time later, Sam turned off the road at a tree that had been split by lightning. He headed down a shallow gulch that was covered with thick grass. Mexico's long legs ate the miles up in no time.

Soon they reached Wild Duck water hole. This was where Sam had to leave the rough trail. He turned right and went up a rocky little hill. The only thing that grew there was cactus.

At the top of the hill, Sam stopped. He took his last look at the land around him. After this, he would be winding through brush and thickets. He wouldn't be able to see more than 20 yards in any direction. He'd be guided only by memory and the sun.

In about two hours, Sam discovered he was lost. Then came the usual confusion of mind and the hurry to get somewhere. Mexico was eager to fix things. The horse twisted and turned through the bushes. For as soon as Sam knew he was lost, Mexico did too.

There were no hills to climb now. So there was no way to see where they were headed. They were lost in the great lonely flats near the bottomlands of the river. It was no great thing for a cowboy or sheepman to be lost. Even for a whole day or a night. In fact, it happened often.

It just meant missing a meal or two. That and sleeping on your saddle blankets or a soft mattress of grass.

But in Sam's case, things were different. Marthy was afraid of the country. Afraid of strangers, of snakes, even of sheep. So Sam had never left her alone at night.

It must have been about four o'clock when Sam got really worried. He was tired and sweaty. Until now he had been hoping he'd find his way. But he must have ridden past the trail he should have taken. He wanted to find a ranch or a camp. Any place where he could get a fresh horse and ask directions. Then he would ride all night to get back to Marthy and the kid.

There was a big lump in Sam's throat. He thought about the cross words he had said to his wife. Surely it was hard for her to live on the ranch. Too hard to have to put up with his complaining. He felt a sudden flush of shame. How could he say such rough things to her for reading?

"It's the only kind of fun the poor gal's got," said Sam aloud. He almost sobbed, which made Mexico jump. "Livin' with a sore-headed old coyote like me. A low-down skunk that ought to be whipped with his horse's reins. Cookin' and washin' and livin' on mutton and beans. And me gettin' riled because she takes a squint or two at a book!"

He thought of Marthy when he first met her. She'd been smart, pretty, and sassy. That was before the sun turned the roses in her cheeks brown. Before the silence of the wilderness had tamed her.

"I'll never speak another hard word to that little gal," muttered Sam. "I'll show her all the love that should be comin' her way. If I don't, may a wildcat tear me to pieces."

He knew what he would do. He would write to the store in San Antonio. He'd have them send down a big box of books for Marthy. Things were going to be different. He wondered about a piano. Perhaps one would fit in the house without the family having to move outdoors.

There was another reason Sam felt bad. That was the thought of Marthy and Randy having to spend the night alone. Sure, Sam and Marthy had words sometimes. But when night came, she'd always forget her fears. She would rest her head on Sam's strong arm and sigh with happiness.

Besides, were Marthy's fears so silly? Sam

thought of the robbers and the sly mountain lions that sometimes snuck onto the ranch. He thought of rattlesnakes, spiders, and a dozen other possible dangers. Marthy would be beside herself with fear. Randy would cry and call for his "dada."

Still, he traveled through endless stretches of brush and cactus. Hollow after hollow, slope after slope—all alike. All the same, yet all strange and new. If only he could get *somewhere*.

The straight line is only found in art. Nature moves in circles. Men lost in the snow travel in circles. They keep going until they get too tired to go on. Their footprints prove this. Also, thinkers often wind up right back where they started.

Just when Sam was filled up with thoughts of how he'd change, Mexico slowed down. The horse sighed, then went from a trot to a walk. They were winding up a slope covered with bushes ten or twelve feet high.

"I say, Mex," said Sam, "this won't do at all. I know you're plumb tuckered out. But we have to git along. Oh, Lordy, ain't there no more houses in this world?" He gave Mexico a sharp kick with his heels.

Mexico grunted as if to say: "What's the use of that? Now that we're so near." The horse sped up a bit. Then he went round a clump of bushes and stopped short. Sam dropped the reins and sat. He was looking into the back door of his own house. It wasn't more than ten yards away.

Marthy was there, calm and comfortable. She sat in her rocking chair in the shade. Her feet rested on the porch steps. Randy was on the ground, playing with a pair of spurs. The little boy looked up at his father. Then he went on playing and singing a little song.

Marthy turned her head and looked at Sam and Mexico. She held a book in her lap with her finger marking the place.

Sam shook himself like a man coming out of a dream. Slowly, he got down off Mexico. He licked his dry lips.

"I see you are still settin' there," he said. "Still reading them stupid novels."

Sam had traveled round the circle. He was himself again.

Jimmy Hayes
and Muriel

Supper was done. Silence had fallen over the camp. The water hole shone from the dark earth like a patch of fallen sky. Coyotes yelped. The dull thump of hooves came from the tied-up horses. Half a troop of Texas Rangers sat around the fire.

The rangers heard a familiar sound. It was thorny bushes rubbing against stirrups. The sound came from the thick brush above the camp. They listened carefully. They heard a loud and cheerful voice call out.

"Brace up, Muriel. We're almost there now. Been a long ride for you, ain't it, you old handful of carpet tacks? Hey, stop tryin' to kiss me! Don't hold on to my neck so tight. This here horse ain't too sure-footed. He's likely to dump us both off if we don't watch it."

Two minutes later a tired pony rode into camp. A tall young man sat in the saddle. The "Muriel" he'd been talking to was nowhere to be seen.

"Hi, fellows!" shouted the rider. "I've got a letter for Lieutenant Manning."

He got off the horse and tied it to a bush. While the lieutenant was reading the letter, he rubbed at some mud on his horse's leg.

"Boys," said Lieutenant Manning, "this is Mr. James Hayes. He's a new member of the troop. Captain McLean sent him down here. The boys will get you some supper, Hayes."

The other rangers greeted the newcomer in a friendly way. Still, they looked him over carefully. They weren't too quick to make up their minds about him. A new member of the troop had to prove himself. After all, your own life might depend on his loyalty, nerve, and aim.

After supper, Hayes joined the others around the fire. He was a tall, smiling fellow. He had yellow hair and a face browned by the sun.

The new ranger started to talk. "Fellows, I want you to meet a lady friend of mine. Ain't never heard anyone call her a beauty. But you'll all see she's got her good points. Come along, Muriel!"

He held open the front of his blue shirt. Out of it crawled a horned frog. A bright red ribbon was tied around her spiky neck. The frog crawled to its owner's knee and sat there.

Hayes waved his hand. "This here Muriel has got quality," he said. "She never talks back. She always stays at home. And she's happy with one red dress for every day and Sunday too."

"Look at that insect," said one of the rangers with a grin. "I've seen plenty of them horned frogs. But I never knew anyone to have one for a partner. Does the thing know you from anybody else?"

"Take her and see," said Hayes.

The ranger took Muriel from Hayes's knee and went back to his own seat. The horned frog twisted and clawed and fought in his hand. After a minute or two, the ranger put it on the ground. The frog hopped on its odd legs and stopped close to Hayes's foot.

"Well, dang my hide!" said the other ranger. "The little cuss knows you. Never thought them insects had that much sense."

Jimmy Hayes soon became a favorite in the ranger camp. He had an endless store of good humor. And he was never without his horned frog. It traveled in his shirt during rides. It sat on his knee or shoulder in camp. It slept under his blankets at night. The ugly little beast never left him.

It was never clear exactly what the feelings were between Jimmy and the frog. We don't know much about a horned frog's ability to care for anyone. It was easier to guess at Jimmy's feelings. Muriel was his best story, and he loved her for that. He caught flies for her. He kept her out of the cold wind. Yet his care was half selfish. And at the end, she repaid him a thousand times. Other Muriels have done the same for other Jimmys.

The other rangers loved Jimmy for his cheerfulness and his stories. But they were still not sure about him. A ranger's life is more than having fun in camp. There are horse thieves to trail and robbers to catch. There are crooks to battle and bandits to find. Jimmy didn't know much about the rangers' ways. So the others all wondered how he would act if things got dangerous.

For two months, everything was pretty quiet. The rangers hung around camp with nothing much to do. And then came some news. Sebastiano

Saldar had crossed the border with his gang. They had begun to rob their way across the countryside. It looked like Jimmy Hayes would soon be able to prove himself.

The rangers took off after the gang. But Saldar and his men were hard to catch. One evening, the rangers stopped for supper. Their horses stood panting with their saddles on. The men were frying bacon and boiling coffee.

Suddenly Saldar and his gang rushed out of the bushes. They fired their six-shooters and yelled. It was a neat surprise.

The rangers got their guns ready. But the attack was only for show. Saldar and his gang galloped off, yelling and firing their guns.

The rangers took off after them. But in less than two miles, the tired ponies had to stop. Lieutenant Manning gave the order to give up and return to camp.

That was when they discovered that Jimmy Hayes was missing. Someone remembered seeing him run for his pony. But no one had set eyes on him after that.

Morning came, but no Jimmy. The rangers searched the countryside. They were afraid he had been killed or hurt. But they didn't find him. They didn't find any sign of Saldar and his gang, either.

Some of the rangers began to wonder. They thought that Jimmy must have run away at the first sign of trouble. He wouldn't return, they figured. He wouldn't want to face his fellow rangers now.

So Lieutenant Manning and his men were gloomy. Having a man run off was a black mark on the troop's record. Never in the history of the rangers had such a thing happened. All of them had liked Jimmy too. That only made it worse. Days, weeks, and months went by. Still a little cloud hung over the camp.

At last, the lieutenant and his men moved on. They camped at many places and rode many miles. Then, nearly a year later, they returned to their old camp.

One afternoon, the men came upon a patch of open land. There they found a scene of terrible tragedy. The bones of three men lay in a hollow. From their clothing, it was easy to tell who they had been. One was Sebastiano Saldar. His hat, covered with gold threads, told them that. The other two were members of his gang. Three guns were resting on a ridge, all pointed in the same direction.

The rangers rode off in that direction for 50 yards. There they found another set of bones. The man's rifle lay beside him. There was no way to tell who he had been. His clothing was like what hundreds of men wore.

"Some cowboy met up with Saldar and his gang," said Lieutenant Manning. "He was brave, though. He put up a dandy fight before they got him. So that's why we never saw another sign of Saldar and his gang."

Then something moved from beneath the ragged clothing of the dead man. Out wiggled a horned frog. It had a faded red ribbon around its neck. It crawled up on what had been the man's shoulder. And so, without saying a word, it told the story. How a young man had gone after a terrible thief and his gang. And how he had died for the honor of the Texas Rangers.

The rangers moved closer. A wild yell rose from their lips. The cry was many things at once. It was a funeral song, an apology, and praise for a hero. A strange service, you might say, over the body of a fallen comrade. But if Jimmy Hayes could have heard it, he would have understood.

The Ransom of Red Chief

The Tale of a Reformed Kidnapper

Bill and I were down South when we got the kidnapping idea. We were in a little town built on land flat as a pancake. So it was called Summit, of course.

Now Bill and me together had about $600. We needed another $2,000 to pull off a scam we had planned. We'd noticed that there were lots of children in town. So kidnapping seemed like a good project.

We picked our victim carefully. He was the only child of a banker named Ebenezer Dorset. The kid was a boy of about ten. He had freckles and hair the color of carrots. Bill and me figured old Ebenezer would pay a ransom for his son. But wait until I tell you.

About two miles from Summit was a little mountain. It was covered with thick bushes. And at the back of the mountain there was a little cave. That's where we put our supplies.

The Kidnapping

One evening we drove a buggy past Dorset's house. The kid was in the street, busily throwing rocks at a kitten.

"Hey, little boy!" called Bill. "Would you like a bag of candy and a nice ride?"

The boy threw a piece of brick and hit Bill in the eye. Bill climbed out of the buggy and took off after him. The kid fought like a bear, but at last we got hold of him. We put him in the buggy and drove off to the cave.

Bill stayed there with the kid while I drove the buggy back to town. Then I walked to the cave. Bill was putting a bandage on the scratches the boy had given him. A fire burned near the cave entrance. The boy stood there with two feathers stuck in his red hair.

"Ha!" the kid said to me. "Paleface, do you dare to enter the camp of Red Chief?"

"We're playing Indian," said Bill, who by then was checking some bruises on his shins. "I'm supposed to be Old Hank, the trapper. I'm Red Chief's prisoner. He's going to scalp me in the morning. Boy, can that kid kick hard."

The fun of camping had made the boy forget that he'd been kidnapped. Right away, he told me my name was Snake Eye. And that I would be burned at the stake at sunrise.

At suppertime, he filled his mouth with bacon and bread and gravy. Then he made an after-dinner speech.

"I like this fine. I never camped out before. But I did have a pet possum. And I was nine on my last birthday. I hate school. Are there any real Indians in these woods? I want some more gravy. What makes your nose so red, Hank? My father has lots of money. Are the stars hot? I don't like girls. Why are oranges round? Have you got beds to sleep on in this cave? How many does it take to make twelve?"

Every few minutes he would remember he was supposed to be an Indian. He'd let out a war cry that made Bill shiver.

I asked the kid, "Red Chief, would you like to go home?"

"What for?" he answered. "I don't have any fun at home. I like camping. You won't take me back, will you, Snake Eye?"

"Not right away. We'll stay here in the cave for a while."

"All right!" he said. "That'll be fine. I've never had so much fun in all my life."

At bedtime, Bill and I put Red Chief between us. He kept us awake for hours. He'd jump up every time there was a rustle outside. He was sure it was an outlaw band sneaking up on us. At last I fell asleep. I dreamed I had been kidnapped by a pirate with red hair.

The Attack of Red Chief

Bill's screams woke me. I jumped up to see what was wrong. Red Chief was sitting on Bill's chest. In one hand, he had a hunk of Bill's hair. In the other, he had the sharp knife we used for cutting bacon. He was trying to scalp Bill!

I got the knife away from the kid and made him lie down. From then on, Bill's spirit was broken. He lay down on his side of the bed, but he didn't go to sleep. In fact, he never closed an eye again as long as that boy was with us.

I dozed off for a while. Then I remembered that I was supposed to be burned at the stake at sunrise. I sat up and leaned against a rock.

"Why are you up so soon, Sam?" asked Bill.

"I have a pain in my shoulder," I said.

"You're a liar!" cried Bill. "You're scared. You're supposed to be burned at sunrise, and you're afraid he'll do it. And he would, too, if he could find a match. Ain't he awful, Sam? Why would anyone pay money to get a kid like that back?"

"Parents love a kid with that kind of spirit," I said. "Now you and the Chief cook breakfast. I'll go check things out."

I went up to the top of the mountain to look out over the road below. I had expected to see the citizens of Summit. They'd be carrying rakes and pitchforks and searching for the terrible kidnappers. But nobody was searching. Nobody was running around. Nobody was bringing news to the sorrowful parents. In fact, the countryside looked downright sleepy.

Perhaps they haven't missed him yet, I thought. I went back to the cave for breakfast.

When I got there, I found Bill pressed up against the cave wall. He was breathing hard. The boy was trying smash him with a rock half as big as a coconut.

"He put a red-hot potato down my back!" explained Bill. "And then he mashed it with his foot. So I smacked him. Have you got a gun on you, Sam?"

I took the rock away from the boy.

"I'll get you!" said the kid to Bill. "No one hits Red Chief. You better beware!"

After breakfast, the kid took a piece of leather out of his pocket. He went outside and started unwinding a string that was tied around it.

"We've got to fix up a plan to get the ransom," I told Bill. "No one seems to know he's gone yet. But he'll be missed today. So we'll send a message to his father. We'll ask for $2,000 for his return."

Just then we heard a war cry. Red Chief was whirling something around his head. The piece of leather he'd taken out of his pocket was a slingshot.

I ducked. There was a heavy thud and a

sigh from Bill. The same kind of sound a horse makes when you take its saddle off. A rock the size of an egg had caught Bill just behind his left ear. He fell in the fire. I dragged him out and poured cold water on his head.

By and by, Bill came to. He sat up and felt the bump behind his ear. "You won't leave me here alone, will you, Sam?"

I went out and caught the boy. I shook him until his freckles rattled. "You better behave," I said. "Or I'll take you straight home. Now, are you going to be good, or what?"

"I was only kidding," he said. "I didn't mean to hurt Old Hank. I'll behave, if you don't send me home. And if you let me play Black Scout today."

"You and Bill talk about it," I said. "He's your playmate for the day. I'm going away on business for a while. Now you come and tell Bill you're sorry."

I made him and Bill shake hands. Then I took Bill aside. I told him I was going to a little village near the cave. I'd see if there was any talk about a kidnapping in Summit. Also, I'd mail a letter to old man Dorset. In it, we'd demand the ransom and tell him how it should be paid.

"I've always stood by you, Sam," said Bill.

"Through fire, flood, and earthquakes. In poker games, police raids, and train robberies. I never lost my nerve until we kidnapped this kid. You won't leave me long with him, will you?"

"I'll be back this afternoon," I said. "You keep the boy busy and quiet until then. Now, let's write our letter."

The Ransom Note

I got paper and pencil and started the letter. Bill begged me to ask for less money. "It isn't human to expect the boy's father to pay $2,000. Not for that forty-pound chunk of wildcat. Let's ask for less. You can take the difference out of my share."

So, to make Bill feel better, I agreed. We worked together to write a letter that went this way:

Mr. Ebenezer Dorset:

We have your boy hidden in a place far from Summit. It's no use trying to find him. There's only one way to get him back. We want $1,500 in big bills for his return. The money should be left tonight at midnight. Put it in the same spot as your answer to this letter. If you agree, send your answer in writing at half past eight o'clock. Tell the messenger to come alone. On the road to Poplar Cove there are three large trees close to the fence. There will be a small box at the bottom of the fence across from the third tree. Tell the messenger to put the answer in the box.

If you try to trick us, you will never see your boy again. If you pay the money, he will be returned safe and well within three hours.

Two Desperate Men

I put the letter in my pocket. As I got ready to leave, the kid came up to me. "Snake Eye, you said I could play Black Scout while you were gone."

"Mr. Bill will play with you," I said. "What kind of game is it?"

"I'm Black Scout," said Red Chief. " I have to ride to the fort to warn the settlers that Indians are coming."

"It sounds harmless," I said.

"What do I have to do?" Bill asked the boy.

"You're my horse. Get down on your hands and knees."

Bill did. Then Black Scout jumped on Bill's

back and dug his heels in.

"Hurry back, Sam," begged Bill. "I wish we hadn't made the ransom more than $1,000. Say, kid, stop kicking me or I'll spank you."

I walked to the village and hung around the post office, talking to folks. One old man said he'd heard that Summit was all upset. It seemed that Ebenezer Dorset's boy had been lost or stolen.

That was all I wanted to know. I checked with the postmaster. He told me someone would be by to pick up the mail in an hour or so. It would reach Summit by late morning. So I mailed our letter.

When I got back to the cave, Bill and the boy were nowhere to be found. I sat down to wait. In about half an hour, I heard a noise in the bushes. Bill staggered out. Behind him was the kid, stepping softly like a scout. Bill stopped and the kid did too.

"Sam, I couldn't help it," Bill said. "I sent him home. The deal is off. There's a limit to what a man can take."

"What's the trouble, Bill?" I asked.

"I was his horse," said Bill. "And he rode me 90 miles to the fort. He fed me sand, Sam. Said it was oats. Then he asked me questions for an hour. I couldn't stand any more. I took him by the collar and dragged him down the mountain. I showed him the road to Summit. And I kicked him eight feet nearer to town. I'm sorry we won't get the ransom. But it was either get rid of him or take me to the madhouse."

Bill was breathing heavily. But he had a look of peace and happiness on his face.

"Bill, there's no heart trouble in your family, is there?" I asked.

"No. Why?"

"Turn around and look behind you."

Bill turned and saw the boy. He turned pale and sat down plump on the ground. Then he started to pick at the grass. For an hour or so, I was afraid for his mind. So I told him we'd get the money that very night. And then we'd be done with the kid.

Bill cheered up enough to give the kid a weak smile.

A Change of Plans

I knew exactly what I was going to do. Before half past eight o'clock, I was up in the tree watching the road. Right on time, a boy rode up on a bicycle. He put a folded piece of paper in the box. Then he rode off.

I waited an hour to be sure it wasn't a trap.

Then I slid down the tree and grabbed the paper. Back at the cave, Bill and I read the note.

Gentlemen:

I got your letter today. I think you are a little high in your demands. So I will make you an offer I think you will accept. You bring Johnny home and pay me $250. I will take him off your hands. You had better come at night. The neighbors won't be happy to see anyone bringing him back.

Yours respectfully,
Ebenezer Dorset

"What!" I cried.

"Sam," said Bill. "What's $250? We've got the money. One more night with this kid will finish me off. I think we're getting away cheap."

"To tell you the truth, this little lamb has gotten on my nerves too," I said. "We'll pay the ransom."

We took the kid home that night. We got him to go by saying his father was going to take us bear hunting.

At midnight we knocked on Ebenezer's door. Bill counted out $250 into the man's hand.

When the kid found out we were leaving

him there, he started to howl. He grabbed hold of Bill's leg and had to be peeled off.

"How long can you hold him?" Bill asked old man Dorset.

"I'm not as strong as I used to be," the kid's father said. "But I think I can give you ten minutes."

Bill took off. He was a good mile out of town before I caught up with him.

The Ransom of Red Chief

The Tale of a Reformed Kidnapper

Cast

Narrator

Bill

Sam

Red Chief

Ebenezer Dorset

Act One

Narrator: Bill and Sam were down South when they got the kidnapping idea. They were in a little town built on land flat as a pancake. So it was called Summit, of course.

Bill: We need to get some money, Sam. We only have about $600 between the two of us.

Sam: I have an idea. Have you noticed that there are lots of children in town? It seems like kidnapping might be a good project.

Bill: Kidnapping? I don't know, Sam.

Sam: Don't worry. I've been thinking about this. I've even picked our victim.

Bill: Who is it?

Sam: He's the only son of a banker named Ebenezer Dorset. A kid of about ten with freckles and hair the color of carrots.

Bill: Do you figure old Ebenezer would pay a ransom for the boy?

Sam: Sure as shootin'.

Narrator: So Sam and Bill started planning. About two miles from Summit was a little mountain. It was covered with thick bushes. And at the back of the mountain there was a little cave. That's where they put their supplies. Then, one peaceful evening, they drove a buggy past Dorset's house.

Sam: There he is.

Bill: Where? You don't mean that kid in the street, do you? Not the one throwing rocks at the kitten!

Sam: That's the one. Now call him over like we said.

Bill: Hey, little boy. Would you like a bag of candy and a nice ride?'

Red Chief: Get lost, mister!

Sam: Look out, Bill! He's going to throw that piece of brick at you!

Bill: Ouch!

Narrator: Now, getting hit in the eye with a piece of brick was enough to make Bill mad. He climbed out of the buggy and took after the boy. Sam jumped out to help. At last they got hold of him.

Bill: Whew, this kid fights like a bear.

Sam: Dump him in the bottom of the buggy. We have to get out of here.

Narrator: They took off for the cave.

Sam: Okay, you stay here with the kid, Bill. I'll take the buggy to town and walk back here.

Bill: Don't be long, Sam.

Narrator: Sam went as fast as he could, but it was a while before he got back to the cave.

Sam: What are you doing, Bill?

Bill: Just putting a bandage on my scratches, that's all.

Sam: And what about the kid? Why is he wearing two feathers in his hair?

Red Chief: Paleface, do you dare to enter the camp of Red Chief?

Bill: We're playing Indian. I'm supposed to be Old Hank, the trapper. I'm Red Chief's prisoner. He's going to scalp me in the morning. Boy, can that kid kick hard.

Red Chief: And your name is Snake Eye, mister. You're gonna be burned at the stake at sunrise.

Sam: Sure, kid. Now let's eat some supper.

Narrator: Bill got to work and soon they sat down to a meal of bacon and bread and gravy. The kid stuffed his mouth, then made an after-dinner speech.

Red Chief: I like this fine. I never camped out before. But I did have a pet possum. And I was ninc on my last birthday. I hate school. Are there any real Indians in these woods? I want some more gravy. What makes your nose so red, Hank? My father has lots of money. Are the stars hot? I don't like girls. Why are oranges round? Have you got beds to sleep on in this cave? How many does it take to make twelve?

Sam: Red Chief, would you like to go home?

Red Chief: What for? I don't have any fun at home. I like camping. You won't take me back, will you, Snake Eye?

Sam: Not right away. We'll stay here in the cave for a while.

Red Chief: That'll be fine. I've never had so much fun in all of my life.

Act Two

Narrator: At bedtime, Bill and Sam put Red Chief between them. He kept them awake for hours. He'd jump up every time there was a rustle outside. He was sure it was an outlaw band sneaking up on the cave. Then, before dawn . . .

Bill: Eeeeeeeee!!!!!

Sam: Huh? What? Why are you screaming, Bill?

Bill: Sam! Help! Get him off of me!

Sam: Red Chief! Put that knife down. And let go of Bill's hair.

Bill: He's trying to scalp me, Sam.

Sam: Give me the knife, kid. Now lie down. And you go back to sleep, Bill.

Narrator: Of course, poor Bill couldn't sleep. And when Sam dozed off, he had a dream. It was a dream that he had been captured by a red-haired pirate. After a while, Sam woke. He sat up and leaned against a rock.

Bill: Why are you up so soon, Sam?

Sam: I have a pain in my shoulder.

Bill: You're a liar! You're scared. You're supposed to be burned at sunrise, and you're afraid he'll do it. And he would, too, if he could find a match. Ain't he awful, Sam? Why would anyone would pay money to get a kid like that back?

Sam: Parents love a kid with that kind of spirit. Now you and the Chief cook breakfast. I'll go check things out.

Narrator: So Sam went up to the top of the mountain to look out over the road below. He had expected to see the citizens of Summit. He thought they'd be carrying rakes and pitchforks and searching for the terrible kidnappers. But nobody was searching. Nobody was running around. Nobody was bringing news to the sorrowful parents. In fact, the countryside looked downright sleepy.

Sam: Perhaps they haven't missed him yet. I might as well go back to the cave for breakfast.

Narrator: When Sam got there, he found Bill pressed up against the cave wall. He was breathing hard. The boy was trying to smash him with a rock half as big as a coconut.

Bill: He put a red-hot potato down my back! And then he mashed it with his foot. So I smacked him. Have you got a gun on you, Sam?

Red Chief: I'll get you, Hank! No one hits Red Chief. You better beware!

Sam: Give me the rock, kid. Now, come on, Bill. Let's eat.

Narrator: After breakfast, the kid went outside. He took a piece of leather out of his pocket. Then he started to unwind a string that had been around it.

Bill: What's he doing now, Sam?

Sam: Don't worry about him. We've got to fix up a plan to get the ransom, Bill. No one seems to know the kid's gone yet. But he'll be missed today. So we'll send a message to his father. We'll ask for $2,000 for his return.

Red Chief: Woo-woo-woo-woo!

Sam: Look out! The kid's got a slingshot!

Bill: Oooh . . .

Narrator: There was a sigh from Bill. The same kind of sound a horse makes when you take its saddle off. A rock the size of an egg had caught Bill just behind his left ear. He fell in the fire. Sam dragged him out and poured cold water on his head.

Sam: Bill! Bill, are you all right?

Bill: What? Who? You won't leave me here alone, will you, Sam?

Sam: Okay, kid, that's it! I'm gonna shake you until your freckles rattle. You better behave. Or I'll take you straight home. Now, are you going to be good, or what?

Red Chief: I was only kidding. I didn't mean to hurt Old Hank. I'll behave, if you don't send me home. And if you let me play Black Scout today.

Sam: You and Bill talk about it. He's your playmate for the day. I'm going away on business for a while. Now you tell Bill you're sorry.

Red Chief: I'm sorry, Old Hank.

Bill: Sorry?

Sam: Come on, now. I want the two of you to shake hands. And then I want to talk to you over here, Bill.

Bill: What do you want to talk about, Sam?

Sam: Come over here where the kid won't

hear us. Look, I'm going to go to that little village near here. I'll see if there's any talk about a kidnapping in Summit. And I'll mail a letter to old man Dorset. We'll ask for the ransom and tell him how to pay it.

Bill: I've always stood by you, Sam. Through fire, flood, and earthquakes. In poker games, police raids, and train robberies. I never lost my nerve until we kidnapped this kid. You won't leave me long with him, will you?

Sam: I'll be back this afternoon. You keep the boy busy and quiet until then. Now, we have to write our letter.

Bill: Let's ask for less money. Please, Sam. It isn't human to expect the boy's father to pay $2,000. Not for that 40-pound chunk of wildcat. Let's ask for less. You can take the difference out of my share.

Sam: Fine. If that's what you want.

Narrator: The two of them worked together to write their letter.

Sam: Okay, listen to this:

Mr. Ebenezer Dorset:

We have your boy hidden in a place far from Summit. It's no use trying to find him. There's only one way to get him back. We want $1,500 in big bills for his return. The money should be left tonight at midnight. Put it in the same spot as your answer to this letter. If you agree, send your answer in writing at half past eight o'clock. Tell the messenger to come alone. On the road to Poplar Cove there are three large trees close to the fence. There will be a small box at the bottom of the fence across from the third tree. Tell the messenger to put the answer in the box. If you try to trick us, you will never see your boy again. If you pay the money, he will be returned safe and well within three hours.

Two Desperate Men

Bill: It sounds good, Sam. Now mail it so we can get rid of the kid.

Sam: Here he comes. I'd better get on my way.

Red Chief: Snake Eye, you said I could play Black Scout while you were gone.

Sam: Mr. Bill will play with you. What kind of game is it?

Red Chief: I'm Black Scout. I have to ride to the fort to warn the settlers that Indians are coming.

Sam: That sounds harmless.

Bill: What do I have to do?

Red Chief: You're my horse. Get down on your hands and knees.

Bill: Okay, I'm doin' it. Hurry back, Sam. I wish we hadn't made the ransom more than $1,000. Say, kid, stop kicking me or I'll spank you.

Act Three

Narrator: Sam walked to the village and hung around the post office, talking to folks. One old man said he'd heard that Summit was all upset. It seemed that Ebenezer Dorset's boy had been lost or stolen. That was all Sam wanted to know. The postmaster told Sam someone would be by to pick up the mail in an hour or so. It would reach Summit by late morning. So Sam mailed the letter. Then he went back to the cave.

Sam: Bill? Where are you? Red Chief? Where is everyone? I guess I'll just sit here and wait.

Narrator: In about half an hour, Sam heard a noise in the bushes. Bill staggered out. Behind him was the kid, stepping softly like a scout. Bill stopped and the kid did too.

Bill: Sam, I couldn't help it. I sent him home. The deal is off. There's a limit to what a man can take.

Sam: What's the trouble, Bill?

Bill: I was his horse. And he rode me 90 miles to the fort. He gave me sand. Said it was oats. Then he asked me questions for an hour. I couldn't stand any more. I took him by the collar and dragged him down the mountain. I showed him the road to Summit. And I kicked him eight feet nearer to town. I'm sorry we won't get the ransom. But it was either get rid of him or take me to the madhouse.

Sam: Bill, there's no heart trouble in your family, is there?

Bill: No. Why?

Sam: Turn around and look behind you.

Bill: No! No! Tell me it isn't so!

Narrator: Poor Bill turned pale and sat down plump on the ground. Then he started to pick at the grass. For a while, Sam was afraid for his mind.

Sam: Bill, it's all right. We'll get our money tonight. And then we'll be done with the kid.

Bill: Do you mean it, Sam?

Narrator: Sam knew exactly what he was going to do. Before half past eight o'clock, he was up in the tree watching the road. Right on time, a boy rode up on a bicycle. He put a folded piece of paper in the box. Then he rode off.

Sam waited an hour to be sure it wasn't a trap. Then he slid down the tree and grabbed the paper. He ran all the way back to the cave.

Sam: Bill! Old man Dorset sent a note. I'll read it. Just listen!

Gentlemen:

I got your letter today. I think you are a little high in your demands. So I will make you an offer I think you will accept. You bring Johnny home and pay me $250. I will take him off your hands. You had better come at night. The neighbors won't be happy to see anyone bringing him back.

Yours respectfully,
Ebenezer Dorset

Bill: An offer . . .

Sam: What?!

Bill: Sam, what's $250? We've got the money. One more night with this kid will finish me off. I think we're getting away cheap.

Sam: To tell you the truth, this little lamb has gotten on my nerves too. We'll pay the ransom.

Narrator: They took the kid home that night. They got him to go by saying his father was going to take him bear hunting. It was midnight when they knocked on Ebenezer's door.

Ebenezer: Who's there?

Sam: We brought your kid back, Mr. Dorset. Open the door.

Ebenezer: Where is my money?

Bill: Here. It's $250, just like you said. Count it if you want. But take this kid off our hands now.

Red Chief: You're leaving me here? No! I want to stay with you, Old Hank.

Bill: Hey, let go of my leg, kid!

Sam: How long can you hold him, Mr. Dorset?

Ebenezer: I'm not as strong as I used to be. But I think I can give you ten minutes.

Narrator: Bill took off. He was a good mile out of town before Sam caught up with him.